KU-253-595

Contents

Note about the story

The One Memory of Flora Banks (2017) is about a 17-year-old girl called Flora Banks who has a problem with her **brain*** called **anterograde amnesia**. This means that Flora can't remember anything that she does or anyone that she meets for very long. Flora writes notes to herself – in her notebook, on **Post-it notes** and on her hands and arms – to help her remember things. After a few hours, Flora's **memories** usually disappear, but one day she kisses a boy and, amazingly, she can remember it. The story follows Flora's adventures as she tries to find the boy who kissed her and **find out** why she still has that one memory.

Before-reading questions

1 Read the "Note about the story" above. What is different about Flora Banks? What is her "one memory"?

2 Flora lives in Penzance, which is in Cornwall in England. Look online and find out information about Penzance. What did you learn?

3 Look quickly at the pictures in the book. What kind of people appear in the story? In what types of places does the story happen?

*Definitions of words in **bold** can be found in the glossary on pages 93–96.

THE ONE MEMORY OF FLORA BANKS

EMILY BARR

LEVEL

RETOLD BY HANNAH DOLAN
ILLUSTRATED BY JULIA CASTAÑO
SERIES EDITOR: SORREL PITTS

PENGUIN BOOKS

UK | USA | Canada | Ireland | Australia
India | New Zealand | South Africa

Penguin Books is part of the Penguin Random House group of companies
whose addresses can be found at global.penguinrandomhouse.com.
www.penguin.co.uk www.puffin.co.uk www.ladybird.co.uk

Penguin
Random House
UK

The One Memory of Flora Banks first published by Puffin Books, 2017
This Penguin Readers edition published by Penguin Books Ltd, 2021
001

Original text written by Emily Barr
Text for Penguin Readers edition adapted by Hannah Dolan
Original copyright © Emily Barr, 2017
Text copyright © Penguin Books Ltd, 2021
Illustrated by Julia Castaño
Illustrations copyright © Penguin Books Ltd, 2021
Cover image copyright © Penguin Books, 2017
Post-it® is a trade mark belonging to 3M Company.

The moral right of the original author has been asserted

Printed and bound in Great Britain by Clays Ltd, Elcograf S.p.A.

The authorized representative in the EEA is Penguin Random House Ireland,
Morrison Chambers, 32 Nassau Street, Dublin D02 YH68

A CIP catalogue record for this book is available from the British Library

ISBN: 978–0–241–52076–5

All correspondence to:
Penguin Books
Penguin Random House Children's
One Embassy Gardens, 8 Viaduct Gardens,
London SW11 7BW

MIX
Paper from
responsible sources
FSC
www.fsc.org
FSC® C018179

Penguin Random House is committed to a
sustainable future for our business, our readers
and our planet. This book is made from Forest
Stewardship Council® certified paper.

CHAPTER ONE
The party

The music is too loud and the room is too crowded. There are more people in this house than any human could possibly know. I have been standing on my own in the corner for some time. I take a deep breath and start to push my way through strangers.

I look at my hand. **PARTY**, it tells me, in thick black letters.

The air in here smells strange. I want to smell the sea. The sea is outside of this house.

"Hi, Flora," says someone. I don't **recognize** him. He is a tall, thin boy with no hair.

"Hello," I say back. I try to look normal. The boy is wearing jeans. All the boys here, and most of the girls, are wearing jeans. I am wearing a white dress with a pair of yellow shoes that don't fit me very well. I probably dressed for what I thought a party was like.

I look at my hand. **I am 17**. I look down at myself again. I am a teenager, but I don't feel like one.

When I was younger, I loved dressing up to go to parties. People told me that I looked like a princess in my party dresses. But I am too old for that now. I want to write that on my arm: "I am older than I think". I should not wear party dresses now. I should wear jeans.

"Do you want a drink?" asks the tall boy.

He is nodding towards a table that has bottles and paper cups on it. I look at my arm. **Don't drink alcohol**, it says.

"Just water, please," I say. My arm also says that **Drake is leaving. P's boyfriend.** This party is happening because Drake is leaving. "P" is Paige. Paige's boyfriend is leaving. Poor Paige.

The tall boy gives me a cup of water. I feel better holding a cup – everyone here is holding cups. I move through the crowd of people, looking for Paige.

I am 17. This is a party. Drake is leaving. Drake is Paige's boyfriend.

A woman puts a hand on my arm and stops me. I turn to look at her. She has blonde hair, and she is older than most of the people at the party. She is Paige's mum. I don't know why, but she doesn't like me.

"Flora," she shouts over the music. She is smiling with her mouth but not with her eyes. "Flora, you're here and you're all right."

"Yes," I shout back, nodding.

"I'll tell your mother," she says. "She's already texted me three times to check on you."

"OK," I say.

"I'm going out now. Will you be all right? I know that you always need a lot of help," she says.

She is being unkind. She looks at me, then she walks away. That woman is Paige's mum, and this is her house.

The people around me are jumping around and doing the kind of dancing that I could not possibly copy. They seem very pleased with the new jumpy song.

"Put the Pixies back on!" someone shouts, close to my ear. I jump and drop water down the front of my dress.

I need to leave and get away from here. Parties are not the way that I thought they were, with princess dresses and games and cake. I can't see Paige. I have no one to talk to.

I am walking towards the door and the smell of the sea, when the music stops and people stop talking. It sounds like someone is hitting a glass with a spoon. I turn towards it.

The person with the glass is standing on a chair. This is Drake. He is Paige's boyfriend, and Paige is my best friend. I met Paige when we were four and started school for the first time. We were both very nervous. I remember the games that we used to play in the playground. I remember helping her to learn to read. I helped her with her school work, and she found us trees to climb.

I see Paige near Drake. When I look at her, I am surprised that she is an adult. Drake has dark hair and thick black glasses.

"Hi, everyone. Thanks for coming," Drake tells this room full of people, "and thank you for having this party for me. I've only been in Penzance for five minutes! Well, five months actually. It's been amazing staying with Aunty Kate and Uncle Jon. It's been great making so many new friends here. If any of you want to come to Svalbard and visit me in the most amazing place on Earth, please do it. I've dreamed of living in Svalbard for *ever*. I feel so lucky to be going to Svalbard."

Someone behind me says quietly, "Can he say 'Svalbard' any more times?"

Someone with them laughs.

I have a phone in my hand. I use it to take a photo of Drake to **remind** me why I am here. I don't know what Svalbard means. It is a strange word but I can see that Drake likes it.

"Of course," Drake says, "while I was here, I was lucky enough to meet the lovely Paige." He stops and smiles and goes a bit red.

"And through her," Drake continues, "I met lots of you. I'll miss you. I'll always remember Penzance, and Paige. Anyway, I'll put lots of snowy pictures online for you all. Thanks to Paige and her parents for letting us have a party in your house. Thanks, everyone!"

People start clapping, and Drake steps down from the chair. Paige looks over at me. She gives me a look that means "Are you OK?" and I nod that I am.

Paige is beautiful, with long, thick black hair and creamy skin. Today she is wearing a dress that is bright blue and short, and she is wearing it with heavy black boots. I look again at my stupid white "party" dress and try not to look at my horrible shoes. I feel all wrong.

I walk as quietly as I can through the side door, but nobody notices me leaving. The cool air hits me in the face, and the sea fills my ears and chest. I close my eyes for a second. **Thank goodness** I am out of there.

———

I am standing in the middle of the road, and it is night. A car comes towards me and makes a loud noise, then it disappears down the dark road. I should not be out on my own. Why am I out in the dark? Why am I alone? Where is my mum?

I am ten years old. I don't know why I am in an adult's body. I hate it, and I want to go home. I run across the road to the beach.

I look at my hand. **FLORA**, it says, and that is me. Under that, it says: **be brave**. I don't know why I am here, but I will be all right.

I am 17, it says.

On my other hand it says: **PARTY** and **Drake is leaving. P's boyfriend**. On my arm it says: **Mum and Dad: 3 Morrab Gardens**.

I know that I have parents, and I know where I live. That is good.

I find a place to sit on the stony sand and stare out at the sea. The sea is black. It mixes with the black night sky. Only the moon lights up the water. I hear someone coming up behind me but I don't look round. Then someone is sitting next to me.

"Flora," says the boy with a big smile.

I look at him. He has dark hair and thick black glasses. I move away from him a little.

"It's Drake," he says. "Flora, are you all right?"

"You're Drake? Paige's boyfriend," I say.

"Yes, I'm Drake. I've known you for months," he tells

me. "And I *was* Paige's boyfriend. We're not together any more because I'm going to Svalbard."

I am not sure what to say to him.

"What are you doing here?" I ask. "Here on the beach."

I look at my left hand. **Drake is leaving**, it tells me again.

He takes my left hand and reads it. "I love the words on your hands," he says. "Do they work? Do they help you to remember?"

Now he is holding both my hands. I like the way his warm hands feel on mine.

The night has got colder, and there is a wind coming straight off the sea and into my face.

"What's it going to be like where you're going?" I ask quickly, because I am uncomfortable.

"It's going to be amazing," he says. "I've been once before, a long time ago. We went on holiday to Svalbard to see the midnight sun. I was ten and I've wanted to live there ever since. Now, after nine years, I'm finally going to do it. My course is taught in English because people go there from all over the world."

He moves closer to me so that we are touching all the way down our sides. I lay my head on his shoulder since I have nothing to lose.

"You're nineteen," I say. "I'm seventeen."

It seems important to remember that.

Drake puts his left arm around me.

"Paige and I broke up," he says.

He turns his face to me and I turn mine to him. When

his **lips** touch mine, I know that this is the only thing in the world that I can do.

Cars go by behind us on the road. The sea moves in and out on the **shore**, close to our feet. I am kissing Drake. I want to sit on the beach with him forever. I don't know how or why this is happening, but I know that it is the only good thing that has ever happened in my life. The rest of the world disappears.

I manage to pull myself back to the real world. The wind makes my hair fly all over my face.

"Hey," he says, "would you like to come to my house?"

I stare at him. I feel uncomfortable.

"But my mum . . ." I say. We stare at each other, and I can't finish my sentence. I cannot look away from his eyes.

"Your mum," he says. "I'm so sorry. That was a terrible idea. I don't know what I was thinking."

He stops talking. I cannot speak, so I nod. I want to write down that I kissed him, right now. But he will think that I am strange if I start writing on my arm while he is talking.

"Flora Banks," he says, "look after yourself. Don't tell Paige about this. Don't tell your mum. Don't write it on your hand."

He picks up a stone from the beach. It is a small, black one.

"This stone is for you," he says.

"I'll keep it forever," I tell him.

CHAPTER TWO

The memory

"You kissed him!" says Paige. She is not shouting, but it would be better if she was. She is quietly angry. "You kissed him. I *know* you did. You won't remember it, but you did it."

Paige is saying words but they are confusing me. I know that she is angry, and I try very hard to listen, but my head is ringing.

"And you've written it down!" One of my **Post-it® notes** is in her hand. The words are there, I wrote them, and she knows that my notes are always true. She knows that this is real.

I know that it is real, too. I can remember it. I remember things from before I was ill, and now I remember kissing Drake. I know, now, that I am not a little girl, because I kissed a boy on the beach. I am not ten. I am 17.

I can remember it. What was it that made me remember? Was it the black stone in my pocket, was it Drake, or was it love? Perhaps this is falling in love.

Maybe I can remember things now. Maybe my **memory** is getting better. But at the moment the only new thing that I can remember since I was ten is kissing Drake.

I look at the note that Paige is holding and see that I wrote the words as small as I could around the edge of it. I wrote: **I kissed Drake. I love Drake.** I am still surprised

13

that it happened. It makes me really happy and it makes me cry.

Kissing Drake is the only clear memory that I have in my head except for the ones from before I was ill. I will do anything to make it stay. I want to live inside that memory as much as I can. I need to keep it forever. If I remember that, I will remember other things. Drake's kiss will be the thing that **heals** me.

Paige is holding the note and staring at me so hard that I have to look at the floor. We are in a café, sharing a pot of tea. Paige saw the note when I took my phone out of my **handbag** to text Mum. A shower of yellow notes fell out of my handbag and Paige helped me to pick them up. I had forgotten that there was something on them that I didn't want Paige to **find out**.

I had forgotten. Of course I had. I remember the kiss, but I had forgotten that I had written about the kiss.

"You *love* him? You actually think that you *love* him?" Paige says. "That's what hurts me the most. Perhaps he kissed you lots of times over the past few months and we don't know about it. I **blame** him for that. He was my boyfriend! If that's the kind of boyfriend you want, you can have him – but he's gone to the Arctic now and neither of us will see him ever again."

Paige stares at me angrily then continues, "You can tell your mum that I won't help her now. Tell her that they will have to take you with them when they go."

I don't know what my mum wanted Paige to help her

with, but now is not the time to ask. I have probably been told twelve thousand times already.

"I'm so sorry, Paige," I say, beginning to **panic**. "We did kiss. We sat on the beach. I didn't plan for it to happen. But I remember the kiss. I actually remember it. In my mind."

"You don't remember the kiss," says Paige. "You have written your little love story down. Every few hours, when you forget everything, you read your notes and tell yourself that you remember it."

She stops and takes a deep breath.

"I've been your only friend for years," she continues. "You have no **freedom** without me. I've taken you out when your mum wanted you at home all day. I take you to the cinema. I take you dancing. Every time you forget where you are, I help you. My mum hates me doing it."

Paige takes a pen out of her bag and starts writing on my yellow Post-it note. When she has finished writing, she **sticks** the note down hard on the table in front of me. Then she picks up her handbag and walks out.

I look at the words on the Post-it note. They now say:

I kissed Drake. I love Drake. This is NOT a secret. I need to find a new best friend. Paige will never speak to me again. Do not call or text Paige ever again.

I drink my tea and stare at the words. I think about the black stone in my pocket.

"I do remember," I whisper to myself. "I do."

When I get home, there is a **suitcase** just inside the door. Mum is not waiting at the window for me. I can hear Mum and Dad moving around upstairs. The house feels busy and different.

"Hello?" I call as I kick off my shoes. I don't know if the suitcase means that someone is coming or going. Maybe we are going away.

Dad comes down the stairs.

"Flora!" he says.

He turns to the stairs. "Annie!" he shouts. "It's Flora!"

My father is funny and lovely. At work, he is very serious. But at home, he wears colourful jumpers that he makes for himself. He would do anything for me, and I would do anything for him – if there was anything that I *could* actually do.

My mother comes quickly down the stairs, almost falling on top of us.

"Flora, **darling**. How's Paige? Why don't we have a cup of tea?" she says.

I really want to tell my parents that I have a memory, but I can't tell them that I kissed Paige's boyfriend. I don't want them to know that I kissed a boy on a beach. My parents are very **protective** of me and, in this house, I am a little girl. It would be wrong to kiss a boy.

"I'll make the tea," I tell Mum.

"Flora," says Dad, when we are sitting at the table with tea and biscuits. "Something has happened. A difficult thing."

I have my notebook and pen in front of me. This feels like something that I need to remember.

Mum is holding her cup of tea in both hands. She doesn't take a biscuit.

"You know Jacob?" Mum says.

"Jacob's my brother. Where is he?" I ask.

I look at the photographs on the wall. There are pictures of me, Mum and Dad. There is a boy in one of the pictures. Our names are under the pictures, and under the boy's picture it says "Jacob (brother)".

I remember Jacob. He is the person that I love most in the world. He used to pick me up and carry me around. I have a very clear memory of him allowing me to paint his toes.

"He lives in France," Mum says. "He's twenty-four now and we don't see him very often. But he loves you very much – more than he loves us."

"Twenty-four?" I say, looking at the picture. That boy is very thin with dark hair and a handsome face. He looks younger than twenty-four.

"That's an old photograph," says Dad. "Jacob called us yesterday. He's very ill. He's in hospital. We have to go to him, Flora."

"We're going to France?" I ask. "That's why there's a suitcase?"

I have never been away from home.

"No," Dad says. "You're not. We're **setting off** tomorrow morning, but we need you to stay here. This is the best place for you."

"But I want to see Jacob! I want to come with you," I cry.

"You can't – you haven't got a **passport**," Mum says. Her voice sounds strange. "If you stay here, you'll be safe.

Paige is going to stay here with you. We'll leave you money and Dad's credit card, and I'll **prepare** meals for you. I'll text you every day when it's time to take your pills. You can take an extra pill every night, to help you to sleep and keep you calm. Paige will be here to help you."

I think about Paige. She won't be here to help me. I still remember that Paige is not speaking to me because she found out that I kissed her boyfriend. Jacob is ill and I want to see him, but I can't because I don't have a passport. If I don't tell my parents about Paige, I will get to stay in this house on my own and I can think about Drake all day. I will be able to sit and remember our kiss. I want to spend as much time thinking about that memory as I can. I don't want it to disappear.

"How long are you going for?" I ask.

"We've booked for five days," says Mum. "I hate to leave you, Flora, but this time we just have to."

I nod and drink my tea.

"When you get back," I say, "can we go to Flambards?"

My mother moves back in her chair and looks shocked. She closes her eyes. Dad puts his hand on top of hers.

"We'll do something fun," he tells me, "I promise."

———————

It is evening and everything is ready. Mum has filled the fridge with food. She has written down which meal Paige and I can eat each day. She and Dad will be home on Saturday.

19

I try to call Paige, but then I see that I have tried to call her five times already. She doesn't answer. Then a text arrives from her:

> Flora, stop calling. I don't want to speak to you. You kissed my boyfriend. Leave me alone.

I don't tell my parents.

I can hear them talking through the door behind me. They are talking in the quiet way they do when they don't want me to hear. I move towards the door and hear Mum say, "No, she doesn't know and let's keep it that way."

My parents are keeping a secret. I write **Mum and Dad have a secret from me** on a note and put it into my pocket. I can look through the house while they're away and try to **work out** what it is.

CHAPTER THREE
Flora's story

I am sitting on the floor of my bedroom, reading a book with a hard cover. On the front it says:

FLORA'S STORY.
READ THIS IF YOU
FEEL CONFUSED.

I think Mum wrote it.

You are Flora Banks, it says.

You are ~~16~~ 17 years old and you live in Penzance in Cornwall. When you were ten a **tumour** grew in your brain and, when you were 11, doctors took it out. Part of your memory went with it. You can remember how to do things (how to make a cup of tea, how to work the shower), and you can remember your life before the illness. But since it happened, you have not been able to make new memories.

You have **anterograde amnesia**. You are good at keeping things in your head for a few hours, and then you forget them. When you forget them, you feel very confused. This is OK: it is normal for you.

21

When you feel confused, you have to look at your hands and arms, your notes, your phone and this book. These things help to remind you of what is happening. You have become very good at writing things down. Your name on your hand makes you feel calm.

You remember us, and your best friend Paige, and other people and places that you used to know until you were ten. You forget other people and places, but that's OK because the people around here know you and they understand.

You'll never live anywhere but Penzance, because this is the only place that you are safe. You will always live with us, and we will always look after you and you will be fine.

You are brilliant and strong. You are not strange.

You will always have everything that you need. You take pills twice a day, and you always will.

Mum xx

I close the book. How could I have forgotten that I have amnesia?

I know that I am 17. I kissed Drake. Everything about that moment is still in my mind – I can actually *see* it. I was sitting on a beach and he came and sat down with me. I was 17 then, and I am 17 now.

My bedroom is the same as it was when I was ten. It is pink and white, with dolls and children's toys.

The words in that book are not true any more. I can

remember something new now, and it is not from before I was ten.

I have kissed a boy, and I am in love. I am 17, and I do not need a little girl's bedroom. That is silly. I pick up some of the dolls, put them into a box and push it into the corner of the room. Those toys belong to a child, and I am not a child.

I sit on the floor and look around me. I could paint this room white, then it would look like a normal room.

I have a memory of sitting on this floor and playing with an ambulance toy. I was a normal little girl. I was talking to my brother, Jacob. He was sitting on the floor with me and helping me to get one of my dolls to hospital. I was happy.

Another memory comes into my mind now. I was getting ready for a day out. It was exciting because we were going to a **fairground**. I was dancing around happily and could not wait to get into the car and go. My family laughed at me and told me that we had to have breakfast first. But I can't actually remember the day out at the fairground. Flambards . . . I remember that it was called Flambards.

The house is very quiet. "Mum?" I shout.

Mum doesn't answer. I think that it must be time for a cup of tea. I run down to the kitchen. I look at the notes stuck all over the walls, and I see why Mum isn't there. She and Dad have gone away, to see Jacob, who is ill.

I start to panic. I can't be here on my own. I need someone. I need my mum and dad. I need people around me.

I run back up the stairs to my bedroom. I can't look at

my parents' bedroom because it reminds me that they're not there. I want to cry.

I know that if I am going to manage on my own, I need to write myself good notes. I turn a page in the "Flora's story" book and write:

Flora's Rules for Life

I try to think of a **rule**, but all I can think of right now is: "Don't panic". I write down:

Don't panic, because everything is probably all right, and if it's not, panicking will make it worse.

I walk from room to room, looking at things. I write longer and longer notes, telling myself why I am alone and how long it will last. I stick them on the kitchen wall.

Mum texts   Take your pills, darling.

I reply   Can we go to Flambards when you're back?

She doesn't reply.

I decide to send a message to Paige because she is supposed to be here with me but I can't find her in the house. When I find her name in my phone, I see lots of texts from her. The last one says:

Flora, stop calling. I don't
want to speak to you.
You kissed my boyfriend.
Leave me alone.

Paige is not my friend any more because I kissed her boyfriend on the beach. I remember it, and I know that it is true.

I stare at a note beside my bed that says **DRAKE** on it. I have drawn a heart around it. I find the black stone and hold it to my lips. Drake gave me the stone. I remember him giving it to me. I remember.

Living on my own is going to be all right.

I lie in bed and read everything that I have written about Drake. He is in the Arctic. I try to think about him there, but all I can see is snow. He is at university in "Svalbard".

I think about what it must be like to be normal. I imagine my mind filled with clear pictures of all the things that actually happened. I could look back on them any time that I wanted. I cannot imagine how wonderful that must be. I hope that when I wake up I will still be able to remember the kiss.

———————

I wake up in the night and sit up in bed, staring around. The house is completely silent. It is very strange.

I go to my parents' bedroom and push open the door. They are not here. They are the people who look after me and they are not here. The clock in their room says 2:40 a.m.

I run down to the kitchen, and I see the notes on the wall. My parents are not here because my brother Jacob is ill. Paige is not here because I kissed her boyfriend, and I remember doing it. I am at home on my own.

I make a cup of tea and go to the computer. I am looking online at Svalbard when I notice a message in my email **account**. When I see the name of the person who sent it, I can hardly breathe.

It is from Drake. It says:

Flora – I can't stop thinking about you.

They are the best seven words in the world.

Drake

I read Drake's seven words to me again and again. I love Drake, and now he has written me this message. He can't stop thinking about me, and I can't stop thinking about him. I can hardly write my reply because I am excited to tell him that he made me remember.

I manage to write a reply and send it. Then I go back to bed and dream of Drake in his strange new home. I imagine him in a snowy place with houses made from ice. I think about what I could send him. Perhaps I will send him some things from Penzance. I will go to the beach and find a second black stone and send him that.

───────

The next day, I wake up late. The sun comes through my curtains and on to my bed. It is 10:45 in the morning.

I feel very confused, and I begin to panic. I read my hand and the notebook beside my bed. I am Flora. I am 17. I was ill when I was ten, and I have anterograde amnesia. I kissed Drake on the beach and now Paige hates me. I am at home on my own.

Last night, Drake wrote to me. "Flora – I can't stop thinking about you."

I go downstairs and look at the computer. I read the reply that I wrote to Drake at three in the morning. It is much longer than his message to me. It says:

> Dear Drake,
> I am so happy to hear from you. I can't stop thinking of you
> either! And this is the amazing thing: I can remember it! I can
> remember talking to you on the beach. I can remember kissing
> you. Every memory I have usually goes out of my head, but the
> memory of our kiss is still there.
> Paige doesn't want to be my friend now because she knows
> about the kiss. I am sad about that but I can understand.
> My parents have gone to France because my brother Jacob,
> who lives there, is ill. Now I'm at home on my own until Saturday.
> That's why I'm on the computer in the middle of the night.
> How is Svalbard?
> Flora

Drake hasn't replied to my message yet, which I sent nine hours ago. He has probably seen it by now and hasn't answered.

I make some coffee and toast, then I take them to the computer and stare at the **screen**. I wait for a reply from Drake. He is the only person in the world now. Perhaps, after his course in Svalbard, he could come back to Penzance. Or we could live in another place together. We could get married. We could look after each other.

Drake has made me remember. I am going to be normal because of him. I have to spend my life with him because he makes my memory better.

The house phone rings and, when I pick it up, I hear, "I'm just checking that you're alive."

"Paige!" I say, but she has gone.

I lie down on the sofa and watch television. Just as I start to fall asleep, the computer makes a noise. I am at the screen in seconds. Drake has replied.

Flora,

Seriously? You remember? That's crazy and amazing.

Have you spoken to a doctor? Maybe your memory is returning.

Are you OK on your own? I hope your brother will be OK.

I'm thinking of you all the time, and I cannot even see you.

Take care of yourself. Remember to eat, and keep remembering!

Drake

I read it again and again. Drake really likes me. I close my eyes and think about that – a 19-year-old boy is thinking about me all the time. I'm not a child any more.

The house changes. It is no longer empty and silent. Everything in it suddenly looks brighter and more beautiful. Drake and I send messages to each other day and night. My words appear on Drake's computer, in the snowy place, and as soon as he can, he answers them.

I would give anything, I tell him, for the chance to kiss you again, and to have you here with me, where I am, right now.

I would give anything, he replies, to wake up beside you.

29

My parents text sometimes and tell me that they're fine, but that Jacob is very ill, and that it is a difficult time for everyone. I reply, telling them not to worry about me. They ask about Paige, but my notes tell me that she hates me now. I tell them that Paige has lost her phone, and I send Mum messages from Paige, **pretending** to be her.

My memory is not better, but I can still remember the kiss. I must keep that memory.

————

I wake up late again the next day with the words "I kissed Drake" in my head. I kissed Drake days ago now, but that memory is still there. It must be because I love him. It could also be because of the stone he gave me on the beach. I need to ask a doctor: perhaps my brain is healing. I will try to find a doctor and ask them – I write down a note about that.

I go downstairs and read my Post-it notes on the kitchen wall, then I read the emails Drake has sent to me. As I look at them, a new one arrives:

Sorry, Flora, I have to go out of town to the **satellite station**. It's up on a mountain so I won't have any internet. Your parents will be coming home soon anyway, so you should get ready for them. I'll email tomorrow.

OK, I reply, You be careful. I love you.

I check the food in the fridge to work out what day it is. My meals for Tuesday, Wednesday, Thursday and Friday are still there, but I know that does not mean that it's Monday.

I pick up the house phone and call a number from a business card on the fridge.

"Hello," says a man's voice. "Pete's Taxis."

"Hi," I say. "What day is it?"

"Today?" he says. "It's Friday, love. Would you like a taxi?"

"No, thanks. Bye," I say.

I put the phone down. My parents are coming home tomorrow.

I run a bath and write **DRAKE** with my finger on the bathroom mirror. Then I write **FLORA** and **be brave**. I put a heart around the whole thing.

After my bath, I clean the house, then I decide to go out and buy some bread.

The air feels strange on my face. I don't think that I have been outside for a long time. It is a warm day, so I go out in a thin dress. I walk up the road, past a big office building to Chapel Street, where there is a small supermarket.

I think of Drake in his cold, snowy place. I have a boy, hundreds of miles away, who loves me. He replies to my messages. His kiss made me remember.

I want to go to the Arctic to find him. I look down at my hand: **FLORA, be brave**, it says.

I buy some bread and a packet of biscuits. I get milk,

too – I don't think we need any, but buying milk feels like something that normal people do.

When I smile at people, they smile back. I feel happy and decide to walk through town. I am enjoying feeling the sun on my face.

I walk through Penzance, looking in shop windows. I look down at myself. I am 17, but I am wearing a little girl's dress. I look like I did when I was ten, only bigger.

I go into a clothes shop and see a huge **fur** coat, which I put on over my little girl's dress. It's too big, but it's like wearing a thick blanket. I look like a woman who is ready for adventure. I look like a woman with a boyfriend.

"It's a great coat, Flora," says the woman in the shop.

How does she know my name? I look at her. She has a round face and short, dark hair, and I don't recognize her at all. I hate not knowing my own past. I hate that she knows me but I don't know her. I buy the fur coat and leave quickly.

CHAPTER FIVE
Jacob

It is Saturday afternoon and I am sitting at the kitchen table with my phone. My parents will text or call soon because it is 2:20 p.m. and their **flight** from France **landed** around ten minutes ago. My notes tell me that. My notes also tell me that my parents went to France because my brother Jacob was ill, but they are coming back now so perhaps Jacob is better.

I kissed Drake on the beach. I still have that memory, and I think about it as much as I can. When I read my notes, I discover again and again that our **relationship** continues. We have written emails to each other, and they are wonderful emails. I love him and he loves me. He has made me remember, and I need to meet him again, to make my brain work again.

I call Mum's phone but she doesn't answer. I decide to leave a message.

"Hi, it's Flora," I say. "Call me when you can. See you soon!"

I write on a Post-it note: **Left a message on their phone**. Then I notice other notes in the kitchen that all say the same thing. I have now left my parents thirty-four messages.

Perhaps they left their phones in France by mistake. They could be driving back from the airport now but they hate driving. Maybe something bad happened on the journey. I read a note that says they have a secret from me. Perhaps the secret is that they are never coming home.

I get out my phone to text Paige, then I see how many times she has told me to leave her alone. That makes me cry.

Mum's last text says:

> See you soon, Flora darling. Look after yourself.
> Remember – pizza today. And take your pills!
> Mum & Dad xxx

My reply was:

> Yes, pizza! Paige and I are doing great.

That is the last text. Where are my parents? I need to find someone to help me.

I email Drake and tell him about my parents. He does not reply. There is nothing from him, and there is nothing from my parents.

————

I think that I have forgotten something but I can't remember what it is. The house is silent. I am alone. My parents are not here but my notes tell me that their plane from France landed hours ago. I start to panic, then I remember Drake and our kiss on the beach. I lie down on my bed and think about that memory – I live it again and again.

Then I turn on the computer and see two messages from Drake in my email account. I am so happy to hear from him that I start crying before I even read them.

I stare at Drake's words:

Flora,
It's Saturday now, so your parents must be home. I hope your brother is OK.
It's wonderful here, but I'm missing you and I still can't stop thinking about you.
Can I come and see you in the holidays?
Drake

His second message says:

Flora – I wrote that message before I read yours. Our internet wasn't working here. Have your parents come back? Maybe they stayed longer with your brother? It's strange that they haven't called you. Let me know how you are.

I write and tell him that my parents have not come back. Then I write again, and again, and again.

———

"They said that they were coming back," I tell the policeman, "but they didn't. They always do what they say."

The policeman behind the desk in front of me does not look very interested in my problem.

"Your parents are visiting your brother and they have not come home on time?" he says to me.

"That's correct," I say.

"Have you called your brother?" he asks.

"No," I reply.

I see the policeman looking at the words on my hand, trying to read them. Then he looks at my face and stares into my eyes for a few seconds. The look on his face suddenly changes.

"Oh, I know who you are," he says. "You've been here before. I'll call someone for you. Do you have a friend or other family around?"

"Paige is my friend," I answer.

"Can you find Paige's number for me? I'll call and ask

her to come and pick you up," the policeman says.

I look at my phone. Paige will look after me. Then I see Paige's last text to me. It says:

> Flora. This is the last time that I'm going to answer. I'm not your friend any more because you kissed my boyfriend. WE ARE NOT FRIENDS. Leave me alone.

I stare at the words. I did kiss her boyfriend. I remember it. He is Drake, and I love him.

I look up at the policeman.

"It's OK, actually," I tell him, then I run home.

"Hello?" I call into an empty house.

I think about who might help me. Maybe Jacob can. I write the words **Contact Jacob** on my arm.

I search through my parents' office for my brother's address. I check lots of boring letters and papers before I finally find a postcard with a picture of the Eiffel Tower on it. I know that that's in Paris. I turn it over and see that it was written for me:

Looking at this right now and thinking of you. You're amazing. Jacob xx

The postcard doesn't have Jacob's phone number or address on it. But he was thinking of me, in Paris. I shut my eyes and tell him that I am thinking of him too. I hope that he knows.

Then I find a passport and amazingly it is mine. I put it in the back pocket of my jeans and write **I HAVE A PASSPORT!** in big letters down my left arm.

After lots more searching, I find an old piece of paper that has an address written on it and the word "Jacob" above it. It says: Jacob, Apartment 3, 25 Rue Charlot, 75003, Paris, France.

I write a letter to Jacob, saying that I am worried because our parents haven't come home. I ask him to call me if he's well enough, or to ask them to call me if he's not. I add my phone number and email address.

I read it back. It sounds normal, I think. Then I run down the road and post it.

I report everything back to Drake and write it all down in my notebook.

All I can do is wait. It is dark now, so I decide to sleep.

———————

When I wake up, it is light outside. I read everything in my notebook and it makes me feel scared, but my only rule for life seems to be that I must not panic. I try to stay calm.

I sent a letter to Jacob. My parents have not come home. Drake is in the Arctic, and I love him.

I go downstairs and look on the computer. There is one new message from Drake:

Hey, have you noticed something? You have been living
on your own for days now. You have freedom.
You can do anything. You are brave.

I *am* brave. I feel happier.
Then I hear a text arrive on my phone.

> Darling, I'm so sorry we are late! Are you all
> right? Please text right now. We can't use our
> phones in the hospital. We didn't get on our
> flight. Jacob became very unwell and we
> couldn't leave. We had to stay with him and
> trust that you were OK with Paige.
> Jacob is still very ill but we will come home as
> soon as we can.
> Love Mum & Dad xxx

My parents are all right! They are still alive, and they
are still in France. It is not like them to forget me – I forget
things, not them. Jacob must be very ill. He is probably
going to die, but they don't want to tell me in a text.

Jacob is my brother and I don't know what he is like now.
The only memories that I have of him are from when I
was very small. I don't know why Jacob went away and
never came back, but I do miss him. He played with me
and picked me up when I was crying. I love him.

I want to see Drake. He thinks that I can do anything.

He can't come to see me yet because he is studying.

I look at a note on my left arm. **I HAVE A PASSPORT!**,
it says.

CHAPTER SIX
An adventure

I find pictures of Svalbard on the internet. I stare at the place, the real place, where Drake is . . .

Then I look at pictures on my phone and see that I took a picture of Drake at a party. I stare at it for a long time. I look at his dark hair and his thick black glasses. My cheeks start to feel hot and I am filled with love for Drake.

He kissed me and made me remember. I remember it all. I remember his smell. I remember the way his lips felt on mine.

I put on my shoes and run down to the beach towards the sea. I look out at the line where the water meets the sky. I can't imagine the world past that line. I can't imagine anything outside of Penzance. I can remember a car ride to a fairground called Flambards when I was ten – I don't remember ever being away from here after that.

I look at my left hand. **STONE**, it says. I find a black stone on the beach. It looks like the stone that Drake gave me, but this one is for him.

When I get home, there is an email from Drake:

Hi Flora,

I'm really sorry but I think that we should stop talking to each other like this. If you were here, things would be different, but you're not. We are too far away, and you can't come here, can you?

I'm happy that you remember our time together. That means a
lot to me. Sorry for everything.
Love, Drake

I read it again, but it still says the same thing. I don't
know how far away Svalbard is but I know that it must be
a long way. I sit with two stones together in my hand. I am
not going to lose Drake.

I find a credit card in a box on the kitchen table, then I
go online, find a flight to Svalbard the next day and book
it. I look up places to stay in Svalbard and book a room for
five nights – that will give me time to find Drake.

Drake said, "You can't come here, can you?" That is a
question, and my answer is, "Actually, I can." I am going to
surprise him.

I feel very nervous, but I have to go to Drake because
he made me remember. His email said that we need to be
together, and we do – he is right.

I prepare to leave and write things down as I pack them
in my suitcase. There are two pairs of jeans, all of my
jumpers and my new fur coat. I check that everything I am
packing belongs to me and not to Mum. I am going to be
myself in Svalbard.

I pack my notebook and "Flora's Story", the book that
I need to remind me of who I am, in my handbag. Then
I write a long note to myself about where I am going and
why, and what I need to do when I get there. I write down
my flight times and numbers, and my passport number.

41

I leave my parents a note saying that I am fine. I text them to say that Paige and I are going to the cinema.

I set off with my suitcase and lock the front door behind me. Nobody looks at me. I am going to do something amazing. I am going to fly to the Arctic to find the man who has made me remember, and nobody knows about it.

I am wearing my fur coat. My notes tell me that I bought it in town the other day. I am hot, and I feel silly, but the Arctic will be cold and anyway, it doesn't fit in my suitcase.

I walk through the middle of town, and I'm almost at the train station when I hear, "Hello, Flora."

I jump and turn around. It is Paige.

"Hi," I say, and I keep on walking.

Paige walks with me. "Nice coat," she says. "Where are you going?"

I cannot tell her the truth. "My parents are in France," I answer, "with Jacob. They went there because he's ill but he's worse than they realized so they've stayed longer."

"I know that," said Paige. "I was supposed to come and look after you but I didn't because you kissed my boyfriend, remember? I have been checking on you every day anyway, but I'll stop now that you're going to France. Are you going to France?"

I want to say "Svalbard" but instead I say, "Yes, I'm going to Paris."

"Are your parents meeting you?" Paige asks.

"Yes," I say.

"Good. Be careful. Are you sure you can do this, Flora?"

"Yes," I say again.

Paige stares at me hard for several seconds, then turns and walks away.

I look down at my hands. They are covered with notes. The word "Spitsbergen" is written in thick black pen. She must know that that is the island where Drake lives, but I think she believed me about Paris.

My train is waiting at the station. My notes tell me that I need to get on to this train and stay on it until I get to London Paddington. That is how my long journey to Svalbard will begin.

The Arctic Guesthouse

Everything below me is white because it is covered with thick snow. There is nothing made by humans anywhere in this land, except for the shadow of an aeroplane. And I am on that aeroplane, with my nose pressed to the window, looking down.

I check my hand. **FLORA**, it says, **be brave**.

It is good to get a window seat on a plane because you always know where you are. I write that down in my notebook, and it becomes my second rule for life.

We are almost in Spitsbergen, the biggest of a group of islands known as Svalbard. Drake is there, and soon I will be too. I am doing the bravest thing of my life. I have been reading my notes on the journey, so right now I know what I am doing.

I look at the ticket that got me on to this plane. It says that today is Sunday. Mum and Dad were supposed to come back yesterday. I'm sure that I waited longer for them than that. Perhaps I panicked and got confused about the time. Maybe I was too quick to go to the police station yesterday.

I will be in Spitsbergen very soon. I have done it, but I don't know how. I am **amazed** at myself. My notes tell me that I went to an airport in London, then I flew to a place called Oslo in Norway. In Oslo airport, I bought a bright red **lipstick**. I will wear it when I'm in Svalbard, because that is the kind of thing that a girl with a boyfriend does.

I changed all of the money from the box on the kitchen table into the right kind of money for Norway. I also have my dad's credit card.

After Oslo, we landed in a place called Tromsø, and that was confusing. I stood in a line of people, went into the airport, then back outside and on to this plane. This is the plane that will take me to Drake, and I am nearly there.

Drake is right. I can do anything.

All of the people on this plane look like they are going to the Arctic. None of them is wearing a dress. None of them has a large fur coat with them. None of them is on a secret journey to meet the love of their life.

The plane gets lower in the sky and everyone prepares to land in Spitsbergen. I look out of the window again. Drake is down there somewhere, and I am coming from the sky to find him.

———

This is a beautiful land. It could be a land in story books. There is snow falling from the sky, landing on my hair and my fur coat. There are mountains all around me, covered in snow. The airport bus just brought me to the small town of Longyearbyen, and I am standing on the edge of it.

I take a pen and write on my hand: **I am in Svalbard**.

Someone is walking up the road towards me, through the thick snow. I see that it is a man, and he is wearing a big thick coat, like everyone here, and heavy snow boots.

He could be Drake.

He could actually be Drake.

Perhaps I told him that I am coming. He has come to find me. I smile, and my smile turns into a laugh. I start to walk towards him, and then I run. I will run into his arms.

This is a wonderful end to my journey. I did a brave thing and it worked. I must always be brave. This is definitely one of my rules for life.

I get very close to the man before I realize that he is not Drake. I look at the man's face – he has red cheeks and light blue eyes. He is not even wearing glasses.

"Sorry," I say to him, "I thought you were someone I know."

"That's OK," he says. "Have you just arrived? Are you staying here?"

I look towards the low building in front of us.

"Yes," I answer. My notes tell me that I am going to stay here. I hope that I'm right.

"Welcome to the Arctic **Guesthouse**," he says. "Follow me."

I follow him inside the guesthouse. He sits down and takes off his snow boots. I quickly kick off my horrible old running shoes. The building is warm and comfortable on the inside, boxy on the outside. The man walks behind a desk and smiles at me.

"Are you Miss Banks?" he asks.

"Yes!" I reply. I am amazing! I can make things happen. I booked this guesthouse by myself.

He hands me my room key across the desk.

"You have booked for five nights," he says. "Could I have your credit card please?"

I pass it to him. "I might not stay for five nights," I tell him. "I'm here to meet my boyfriend, so I might stay with him. But I will pay for five nights, of course."

Drake is my boyfriend. I kissed him on the beach.

"Is your boyfriend studying at the university here?" he asks me.

"Yes," I say. "Do you know him? His name is Drake Andreasson."

"No, I don't think I do," says the man. "He didn't come to the airport to meet you?"

"He doesn't know that I'm coming," I tell him.

The man nods and looks at me. "Longyearbyen is very safe," he says. "But if you have any problems, just tell us and we can help. Remember not to leave town alone because there are **polar bears** here. Always be somewhere with buildings."

He tells me where to go to find my bedroom, which is bedroom number 5. I don't write a big "5" on my arm because I want him to think that I'm normal.

"Good luck," he says. "Breakfast is here at 7:30 a.m."

This might be the first time that I have ever slept in a room that is not my pink bedroom in Penzance. That room is safe and I miss it. This room is strange. There is a snowy mountain outside my window.

I have managed to get myself to the Arctic, but I don't know what time it is. My phone says that it is half-past midnight, but I can't believe that. It should be dark, but the sun is still out. The words "midnight sun" come into my mind. Perhaps I am looking at the midnight sun. That is very exciting.

There is a text from Mum on my phone:

> Is all OK in Penzance? I tried to call the house phone but there was no answer. We are trying to get home tomorrow xxx

I reply: Yes, fine thanks! Hope you are all OK xxx

After I've sent it, I worry that it sounded strange. However, I am strange, so that text probably sounded normal for me.

Mum texts back immediately: Have you taken your pills?

Yes I tell her.

I look around but I can't see any pills. I decide to find Drake first and worry about that later.

I close the heavy curtains in my room. Light still comes in around the edges but it is dark enough. I get into bed and soon my eyes are closing.

Svalbard

There are people shouting. I don't know how they got into our house. Mum and Dad will make them go away. I will stay here in my bed and wait for it to go quiet.

I hear heavy boots on the floor and doors being closed loudly.

I open my eyes and try to stay calm. I am 17 and I kissed a boy on a beach. I have woken in a strange new world. I reach for my notebook.

This is Svalbard! I feel scared to be here, but that doesn't matter, because today I will surprise Drake. I have to find him immediately, because my parents will soon realize that I am not at home. They might be coming home from France today.

According to my notebook, breakfast is sometime around now. My phone says it's 7:30 a.m. I will have some breakfast, and then I will find my boyfriend.

I get up and open the curtains. I can see deep blue sky. I am in the Arctic. Everything looks fresh and clean, and I feel amazing.

I lock my bedroom door and see two boys locking theirs. One of them says "good morning" to me as he passes. They run outside, shouting to other boys. Maybe they were making all the noise.

I go into a big room where people are eating breakfast.

I want to sit with someone but no one is on their own, so I put my handbag on an empty table and go to collect some food.

This is a strange breakfast, but I'm very hungry so I fill my plate. I take dark brown bread, cheese, fish and a few vegetables. I manage to get coffee from a machine and carry it back to my table without dropping it.

Nobody looks at me. I sit down and drink my watery coffee. Then I realize someone is standing opposite me.

"May I sit here?" she says, looking at the seat. I nod and smile. She puts her handbag on the seat and goes to get some breakfast. She wears little round glasses and warm clothes. Everyone here is wearing warm clothes except for me.

"Hi," the girl says, when she returns. "I'm Agi."

"I'm Flora," I tell her.

She has an egg and some fish on her plate.

"From England?" she asks.

"Yes," I say. "Are you Norwegian?"

"No, no. I'm from Finland," she says. "Are you in Spitsbergen alone? I am. Not many of us are alone here."

"I'm here to visit someone," I say.

"Oh, so you are not actually alone?" she says, sadly.

"I am now," I say. "I didn't tell him that I'm coming. I'm going to find him today."

"You came all this way as a surprise? And now you need to find this person?" Agi says.

"That's right," I say. "Why are you here?"

I am pretending to be normal, and I think I'm managing it. This is very exciting.

"Oh, I love to travel. I have a website where I write about the places that I travel to," Agi tells me. "My website is called 'Adventures of a girl on the road'. Today I'm going on a bus around the town."

"That sounds good," I say. "I would like to go, too, but I'm going to find Drake today. I kissed him on the beach and fell in love with him, so I'm going to find him and maybe I won't go home. Maybe I'll stay here with him forever."

I stop and breathe. That did not sound normal.

Agi is eating her breakfast and watching me. She looks at my face for a long time, then she looks at my hands. She sees **FLORA, be brave** and **I am in Svalbard**. I look down at my hands, too, and feel silly.

"Wow," she says, "you are an interesting girl. You must like this boy, Drake."

"I love him," I tell her.

"How will you find him?" she asks.

"I suppose I'll walk into town and ask people if they know him. I know that he studies at the university and is working at a satellite station," I say.

"I can ask people on my bus today. If you don't find Drake, perhaps I will see you here tonight," says Agi.

"I have to find him today," I say.

Agi finishes her coffee and stands up. "I hope you find him. Have a great day, Flora!"

"Thanks," I say. "You too."

I write Agi's name on my arm, and in my notebook I write: **Look for Agi at the guesthouse this evening, if I am there**.

Now I am outside, in my fur coat and running shoes. The sky is a deep blue, with no clouds. The air is cold and clear. Here I am, Flora Banks, walking down the road in the Arctic town of Longyearbyen. I have a map from the guesthouse, and I am walking towards town. I am going to the place where Drake must be, and I will find him. I am excited to see his face when he sees me here.

It takes me twenty minutes to walk into town. I go into a shop that sells things to wear in **freezing** weather and a woman with grey hair and pink cheeks walks towards me. She says something in a language that I don't understand.

"I'm looking for a pair of boots to wear," I tell her in

English, and she immediately starts to show me boots.

"I like these ones," I say, pointing to a brown pair with fur inside.

"I'll get them in your size," says the woman. She is very helpful.

When I pay for them, I ask her, "Do you know a boy called Drake Andreasson? He studies here."

"Drake?" she says. "Have you asked at the university?"

"I'll try that," I say. "Can I wear the boots now?"

"Of course!" she says.

The nice woman gives me a bag for my old running shoes, and I set off for the university to search for Drake.

CHAPTER NINE
The café

I find my way to the university by looking at my map, but all of the doors that I try are locked. I stand and stare at the doors for a long time. This is the place where Drake studies, but he is not here. I look through my handbag and take my notebook out so that I can write this down.

A woman is standing near me, looking at me.

"Do you know Drake Andreasson?" I ask her.

"Maybe. Is he a student here?" she says.

"Yes," I say.

"Have you tried the university apartments in Nybyen?" she asks.

As I write that name down, my phone makes a noise from inside my handbag. When I see a text from Mum I am pleased, but her message confuses me.

> Darling, I hope you and Paige are OK. We are still in Paris. Jacob is terribly ill now. Maybe you could come to Paris?
> I'll call later to make a plan.
> Mum and Dad xxxxxxxxx

I check through my notebook. Jacob is ill in Paris. My parents are with him and my parents think that I am with Paige in Penzance. I live in Penzance, but today I am in the

Arctic. I got here by myself. My last note to myself tells me that I must not leave town on my own because there are polar bears and they are VERY dangerous.

Reading my notes about Jacob brings him directly into my phone, because when I look at my email account, the words Jacob Banks jump out at me. He has sent me an email:

Dear Flora,

Thanks for the letter. My boyfriend brought it to me in the hospital. You introduced yourself to me so formally – you don't know that we still have a relationship. That makes me sad every time. Are you OK? You sound very worried about Mum and your dad not coming home. I'm sorry – I got more ill just as they were leaving to come back to you. But they're fine, so don't worry about them. You're in Penzance with your friend, aren't you? Or have you gone on another adventure? Please reply. I need you to make me laugh during this terrible illness. Ask me lots of questions, like you always do.

Your brother, Jacob xx

I read it again and again. I don't know how he knew that I have gone on an adventure. Have I done it before? No, that can't be right. I have never left Penzance.

I decide to find somewhere warm to sit and write a reply to Jacob. I love Jacob. He told me to ask him questions, so I will. I have a lot of questions.

I feel the two stones in my pocket as I walk. I look at

every person that I pass, but none of them are Drake.

———————

I am sitting at a table in a **cosy** café and a man is standing in front of me. He is looking at me, and he seems to be waiting for me to say something.

"I want to go to Flambards," I think, but I know that is not the correct thing to say now.

"A coffee," I say, because that feels like a better thing to say. "With milk, please."

"Sure," he replies. He has a brown **spot** on the side of his face, and a beard. "Would you like anything to eat?"

I don't know if I am hungry.

"No, thanks," I answer. I look at my hands. I see **FLORA, be brave** and **I am in Svalbard**.

"Am I in Svalbard?" I ask him.

He laughs. "Yes, you are! This is Svalbard," he says.

"Do you know my friend?" I ask, as I show him the picture of Drake on my phone.

The man looks at it. "Yes, I think I have seen him," he says. "Are you OK? You showed me this picture earlier. I'll tell him that you're looking for him if I see him."

"Thank you. Oh, thank you! Could you tell him that Flora is here?" I ask.

"Flora. Yes, of course," he replies.

"Actually, don't tell him that it's me. I want it to be a surprise. Just tell him that someone is looking for him."

I reply to Jacob's email. I love Jacob. He was my world

when I was a little girl. I want him to be a part of my world now.

I write everything that has happened and everything that I feel in my email – I don't leave anything out. I tell him that I kissed Drake on the beach and that I remember it. I tell him that I am in Svalbard. I tell him that I am not sure what is happening in my mind. I ask him why he went away. I ask lots of questions.

Then I reply to my mum. I tell her that Paige and I are fine. Then I send a second text:

> When you get back, can we go to Flambards?

———

I look up and see that everyone has left the café. Only the man with the beard is there, holding some keys.

"I'll pay my bill," I say to him.

"Don't worry, Flora," he says. "You can have it for free."

I thank him and leave. I don't know how he knows my name.

I follow the map out of town. I know where I am (Longyearbyen) and why I am here (Drake) and where I am going (the Arctic Guesthouse). I am walking in the right direction.

Someone is walking behind me. It is the man with the beard from the café. When I look around, he smiles and waves at me. I keep on walking.

I reach the guesthouse and get out my room key. I also

have a note telling me that I am in room 5. As I walk into the front door of the guesthouse, the man with the beard smiles and waves again at me, then he turns and walks away.

My key opens room 5. I lock the door behind me and sit on my bed. This is not my room, but the things in it are mine. This is the new home that I have made for myself. I take all of the notes that I have here and start reading them.

The word "pills" jumps out at me on the notes. I normally take pills, but I have not been taking them. I feel strange. My hands are shaking. I look in the bedroom mirror and see that my eyes look different and my skin is **spotty**. The girl in the mirror is ugly. I don't understand because Mum says that I'm beautiful.

There is a suitcase in the corner of the room. I put it on the bed and pull out everything inside it. There are no pills. I should do something about that, but I don't know what.

It is evening now but it is still light outside. That is the magic of this place, the land of the midnight sun.

I decide to go out looking for Drake again. I put on a fresh jumper and jeans, and some lipstick to make myself feel better about my skin. As I close my door, a man walks past with a towel over his shoulder.

"Hi," he says. "You look very nice for breakfast! Do you have exciting plans today?"

"Breakfast?" I reply, feeling confused. I thought that I

was going out for dinner, but this man thinks that I'm going for breakfast.

"You do know that breakfast doesn't start for another half an hour, right?" he asks.

"Right, I'm a bit–" I say.

"Don't worry. We all get like that here. The midnight sun is so confusing."

I smile at him then walk back to my room. A whole night has passed and I haven't noticed it.

The boat tour

"Yes, he says that it's fine," says Agi, and I pass her some money.

She gives it to a man who is sitting in the driver's seat of a bus. He counts my money and nods. I follow Agi on to the bus and we sit down together.

Agi and I are going on a **tour**. She invited me to go with her at breakfast. I didn't recognize her at first, but she sat down with me and asked me about Drake. I pretended to remember her, and I think that she believed me.

It is a bright, sunny day. I don't think that I have told Agi about my amnesia, so she thinks that I'm normal. I am going to try very hard to be normal today.

I look down at my hand. I have written **Be normal** on it. I see Agi looking at it, too.

"I should also remind myself to be normal sometimes," she says.

Today, I have to find Drake. My parents will get home soon and then they will come here for me. Going on a tour is an excellent way of looking for Drake.

The bus drives us to a big white metal boat on the **bay** beside the town. We are going on a boat tour! I pretend that I am not surprised about that as I follow people on to the boat.

"Isn't this wonderful?" says Agi, as we stand together on

the **deck** of the boat.

We are looking away from the town, across the bay. There are mountains all around us. I can only see one building across the water – a **cabin** on the water's edge. I can see someone there, pulling a small boat up to the shore. The person turns around, walks up to the cabin and goes inside.

"That's a sweet little cabin," says Agi.

"I can't imagine living there," I say.

"I can," Agi says. "Maybe for a year or two. I would like to be there in the winter. I can imagine that it's wonderfully cosy there in the dark months."

"I wouldn't like that," I say.

"Yes," says Agi. "People say that you shouldn't come here in the winter. But I like the dark, cosy days. Our winters are like that in Finland, too."

I write a note in my book, reminding me not to come here in winter.

The boat starts to move and the town of Longyearbyen disappears. The little cabin on the shore is gone. I sit on the top deck and stare at the beautiful snowy **landscape**. The world slows down and almost stops. Everything that I have ever worried about – whether I remember it or not – disappears. There is nothing but this moment. The air is clear, the water is deeply blue, the boat moves silently across the freezing bay.

I do not talk to people. I just smile, breathe and look at everything around me. This is the Arctic.

A long time passes. The man from the boat has been

talking to people on the journey but I haven't been listening.
Suddenly he says, "Look – there's a **seal**!"

I get my phone out and take pictures of a big, lazy seal
with a funny face. He is lying on a large piece of ice near
the boat. He turns round, looks straight at us, then rolls
off the ice to go for a swim. I want to tell Jacob about him.
Jacob would love him.

"Look!" someone calls out from across the boat. "Bear!
Bear!"

We all turn to look. Moving across the ice between the
boat and a mountain is a big polar bear with two **cubs**.

I take some pictures, then I put my phone away and just stare at them. These animals are dangerous. I know that because it is written on my arm and in my notebook. But they are also beautiful. They don't seem to notice the boat full of people staring at them. They don't care because they are happy in their world.

I know that that mother would do anything to **protect** her cubs. Anything at all.

I HAVE SEEN POLAR BEARS, I write on my left hand.

I see Agi watching me. "You write on your hands a lot," she says.

"Yes – people do that a lot in England," I tell her.

Hours later, we are coming back towards the town, and I don't want to. I like it on this boat, where the seals and the polar bears are. I want to stay here with Agi and the other people on the boat. I'm happy here.

"Flora," says Agi, pointing. "There are some **satellite dishes**. You said that your boyfriend works at a satellite station."

I look across the water and see a building with several satellite dishes at the top of a mountain.

"My boyfriend," I say, feeling confused. I stare at my hands, but they only tell me to be normal and that I saw polar bears. Then I see the word "Drake" and it jumps off my skin.

I could be looking at the place where Drake is, and he is the man that I love. I have just spent a whole day on a boat instead of looking for him. I know that I was on a beach with Drake, but the memory of our time together is starting to disappear.

I start to feel very sick and move to the side of the boat.

"Flora," says Agi. "Are you OK? What is it? I'm sorry if I said something to hurt you. I realize that things might not be good between you and Drake. You went to look for him two days ago and he isn't with you."

I take a deep breath. We are nearly back on land. I want to scream and shout and throw myself off this boat. I want to swim across the bay and climb the mountain to the satellite station to find Drake. But I won't do that. I will stay here and walk calmly off this boat, then I will run away and find Drake. I will find him even if I have to fight past the polar bears.

I am the first person off the boat.

"I'm going to find Drake," I tell Agi, then I run down the road as fast as I can.

———————

Now I am in the snow, standing in the middle of a road, feeling the sun on my cheeks. There is an animal standing on the snow beside the road. It has white and brown fur. I think it is a **reindeer**.

"Where's Drake?" I scream at it. It looks at me, then turns round and walks off.

I follow the reindeer. I walk easily across the snow in my heavy boots. The reindeer goes towards the mountain with the satellite dishes on it and I start walking up it too.

"Drake!" I shout, as I go.

Something about this feels wrong. I look at my arm and see the words **Don't leave town! POLAR BEARS**. I stop and look around. I can't see any polar bears, so it's probably all right.

On my left hand, it says **I HAVE SEEN POLAR BEARS**. That means that I have seen them and I am still alive. That makes me feel better.

I will just walk a little way up the mountain and then I will go back to the town. If I look everywhere that I can, I will find Drake.

———

Now I am on the side of the mountain, and I am freezing. In front of me, there is a snowy, rocky landscape. There are no trees or houses here. There is no Drake.

My phone makes a noise in my pocket. There is a text from Jacob. He is my brother. It says:

Please read your emails.

The cabin across the bay

I wake up in a room with two beds in it, and there is a person sleeping in the other one. I don't recognize her. There is a little table between our beds with several books on it. They are in a strange language that I can't read.

Agi! This woman is called Agi and she is my friend. I *do* know her. I am amazed at myself for knowing that.

That is why I love Drake – he kissed me on a beach and made me remember. Perhaps I am starting to remember more things now. Perhaps my brain is healing.

My phone is next to me on the table. I pick it up and look at it. There is an email from my brother, Jacob, on it:

Baby sister,

You never fail to surprise me. You're in the Arctic! What an amazing adventure.

Are you still taking your pills? If you are, STOP taking them right now. You won't remember this, but you have stopped taking them before. Last time, you went a bit crazy for a few days and your skin became spotty, but after that you looked fine and you were happier.

I have some bad news for you: Steve, your dad and my **stepfather**, is on his way to find you RIGHT NOW! Mum started worrying when she didn't hear from you yesterday. She checked Dad's credit card account and worked out where you are in about two seconds. So they know that you're on an Arctic adventure to find a boy.

They have, of course, called the police, so if Dad doesn't find you, the police probably will. Mum is extremely protective of you. She'll always want to keep you where she can see you, so enjoy any freedom you have now.

I don't have much time left. I hate it. I don't want to die. I'm only 24 years old, and I'm angry about it but I want to think about you now.

You asked me why I ran away to Paris. It was because I hated seeing how our parents treated you. They give you pills to make you calm and sleepy instead of letting you be yourself. They tried to stop me from speaking to you but I always found a way to reach you.

We speak often, Flora – in emails, phone calls and letters. We have a great relationship and we've had some wonderful times, my darling. You're my world. I hope I get to see you again, but if not, it's been amazing. Thank you for everything.

Jacob xxxx

I love Jacob and he is dying. I have run away before. Mum and Dad have lied to me for years. I can't trust them. I need to find Drake because my dad or the police will be here soon and they will take me home. I take a pen and write **Dad is coming** on my arm.

There are lots of texts and emails from my parents, but I don't read them. The clock on my phone says that it is 5:10 in the morning. I sit up in bed. I am still in my clothes from yesterday. My fur coat is at the end of the bed and my handbag is on the floor. I pick up my things and walk quietly to the door.

———————

Now it is eight o'clock and I am standing on a street in town. The woman from the shop where I got my boots from arrives for work. According to my notes, she was nice to me when I bought my boots. She told me to go to the university to look for Drake. I hope that she can help me again now.

The woman stops and looks surprised when she sees me.

"Flora!" she says. She has kind eyes and grey hair. "What are you doing out here? I will call the guesthouse and get Agi to come and collect you."

"I need your help with one thing before you do," I tell her.

"OK, let's talk. I'm Henny. Coffee?" she says.

"Yes, please, Henny," I say.

I follow her into the shop.

While she makes us a drink, I tell her what I need help with.

"My dad is coming here to collect me soon," I say, "but I want to try one last time to find Drake – the boy I came here to see."

"Right," Henny says.

She hands me a mug of coffee. "Now, Flora," she says, "this town is very small and most people who live or visit here talk to and help each other. Everyone is very worried about you. I don't really know Drake, but I can tell you that he is here in town. Toby from the café saw him a couple of days ago and told him that there was a young woman here looking for him. Drake was very surprised."

Henny stops and takes a deep breath.

"Drake told Toby that he has a girlfriend here. Toby wanted to tell you, but he was worried about hurting you. Drake's girlfriend is called Nadia. She is a little older than him. They study here together."

"Drake has a girlfriend?" I say. "But I'm his girlfriend."

"I'm sorry, darling," Henny says.

Drake was Paige's boyfriend, but then I kissed him on a beach and now he is mine.

"Where does Drake live?" I ask Henny.

"Nadia lives in a little cabin across the bay," Henny says. "She comes across to town in a boat every day. Drake spends a lot of time there with her, I understand."

"She lives across the water?" I say.

"Yes – it's the only cabin on that side," replies Henny.

"So Drake is there right now?" I ask.

"I don't know," says Henny. "Listen, we'll call Nadia and ask Drake to come here to talk to you."

I have stopped listening. Maybe Drake *has* started another relationship, but I want to go to him and look him in the eye. I cannot go home without doing that.

I run out of Henny's shop and down towards the bay. She calls after me but I do not stop. There are plenty of little boats on the bay. I get into one and start **rowing** in the direction of the only cabin across the water – the cabin that I saw on my boat tour.

I am on a bay in the Arctic, rowing towards Drake, the love of my life. I am actually doing this. I am being brave.

There is another boat on the opposite shore of the bay. I row my boat up next to it. I cannot stop to worry or think about anything. I walk up to the cabin and knock on the door.

I can hear people moving inside the cabin, then the door opens slowly and he is in front of me: Drake Andreasson, the love of my life.

I start crying immediately and run into Drake's arms. But he doesn't kiss me on the lips. He doesn't look pleased that I am here. He doesn't even look at me. He pushes me away and closes the door in my face.

I stare at the door. People are shouting behind it – I can hear Drake's voice and a woman's voice. I don't know what to do, so I stay where I am and wait.

When the door opens again, a beautiful woman is standing there instead of Drake.

"Hi," she says to me. Her voice sounds American and she has long straight hair. "Would you like to come in?"

I go inside with her and Drake is there, but he isn't looking at me. The living room is warm and cosy. The walls are painted dark red. There is music playing.

"She's crazy," he says to the woman. I try to pretend that he didn't say that. How is everything going so wrong? I remind myself that Drake kissed me and wrote beautiful words to me.

I take a deep breath. "Drake," I say, "I came here to find you because I love you and you love me. You kissed me on the beach. I remember. You made me remember."

"Flora, this is crazy," Drake says. He still won't look at me. "Toby in the café told me that you were in town, but I couldn't believe it. Do your parents know that you're here?"

"Yes," I reply. I take one of the black stones out of my pocket. "Drake, don't you remember? You kissed me and you gave me this stone. You wrote me beautiful emails."

"I didn't do any of that, Flora!" he shouts. He is walking up and down the room. "You imagined it all. None of it actually happened!"

"Drake, don't shout at her!" Nadia says.

She pushes past Drake and puts an arm on my shoulder. She takes me to the sofa and tells me to sit down. I notice that I am crying.

"I think you are very brave to come here, Flora," Nadia says.

"Drake is lying," I tell her. "He did kiss me. I remember it. Then he wrote emails to me."

"I have never sent you a single email," Drake says.

I suddenly feel very angry. "Then who sent them all?" I shout.

"Flora," says Drake, angrily, "you probably wrote the emails yourself, pretending to be me! It was a terrible idea to come here. I'm calling the police right now."

I get up and run out of the front door. Neither of them tries to stop me.

CHAPTER TWELVE

The mountain

I cannot go back to town, so I run the other way instead, up the mountain behind the cabin.

I know that I have done something terrible but I don't know what it is. A minute ago I knew, but every memory that I had from the last few hours has now disappeared. I know that I don't want to go back, but I don't know why.

I am standing on a mountain in an impossibly beautiful, icy place. Far below me is a bay with two boats and a cabin on the shore. Behind me are mountains, as far as my eyes can see. This is the Arctic.

I take two black stones out of my pocket. I don't know why they are there but something tells me that they are important. I throw the stones into the snow, and I immediately feel happier. I sit down in the snow. I want to stay here, alone in this freezing place, forever.

"Flora!" I can hear someone calling my name. I don't know who they are, but I do know that I don't want to see them.

"There you are!" he says.

It is a man, but it is not Drake. I turn and look at him. I don't recognize him. He has a beard and a brown spot on his face.

He stands up and shouts something down the mountain in a strange language. He looks around and then sits down next to me.

"Let's go, Flora," he says to me gently. "You can't sit here. It's not safe. You don't want to die out here, do you?"

I don't move.

"Perhaps you do want to die," he says, looking nervously around him, "but I don't. And I don't want the people who are out looking for you to die either. There are polar bears here. There are terrible stories about what they do to people. So let's go down this mountain to somewhere warm."

I shake my head. "I'm staying here," I say.

"Do you remember me?" he asks.

"No," I reply, quickly. I don't want to pretend any more.

"I'm Toby. I've made you lots of coffee. I've seen you every day for the last four days," he tells me.

I don't look at him.

"Your life is difficult, Flora" he says. "You fell in love but things didn't **work out** as you planned. That's normal – you're normal. We all get hurt and do crazy things sometimes. Now please come down and talk. There are people here who care about you."

"I can't," I say.

"You can, Flora," he says, directly. "I will carry you if I have to."

"I'm not a little girl!" I cry.

But I *am* a little girl. I have been a little girl all my life.

"I think you're amazing, Flora," he tells me. "You got yourself to the Arctic to find a boy. You are someone who gets things done. Yes, you have amnesia, but you are alive! But you might not be for long if you stay out here. It's too dangerous for you to be here."

"I'm not normal. I can't do anything because I forget everything. I don't know what I'm doing here," I say.

"Here's what I see," he says. "I see a girl whose brain has been badly damaged. I see someone who has been shut away by her parents because they want to keep her safe. But inside her is a traveller, who came here not to find Drake, but to find herself. You're the bravest person I know, Flora!"

I finally look at him. "You're just being nice," I say.

"It's true. But now, please stand up and walk with me because there are polar bears close to here and they can run very fast. We must go immediately."

The man helps me down the mountain and when we reach the door of the cabin, he pushes me inside.

"This is Drake's house," he says. "You wait here. Five people are still out looking for you – I need to find them."

He turns around and goes back up the mountain.

I stand in the house. Drake's house. Does that mean that

Drake is here? I really hope that I haven't got anyone killed by doing stupid things.

After a few minutes, the door flies open and two women come in. I don't recognize them. One of them is wearing glasses. She runs to me and puts her arms around me.

"Flora! Thank goodness you're back," she says. "It's me, Agi. I'm your friend."

The other woman has long straight hair. She is holding a gun. She puts it in a cupboard and locks it.

"There are polar bears," I tell them. "They are extremely dangerous."

"Yes," says the woman with straight hair. "It's OK. Toby knows what he's doing out there. Come and sit down."

The next person through the door is Drake. The person that I have come to Svalbard to see. I walk towards him. He is going to heal my memory and make everything better.

"Drake!" I whisper.

He looks at me and I can see that he is scared of me. He puts a hand on my arm and leads me to the sofa.

"Flora," he says. "You don't remember, do you?"

I shake my head. "You kissed me on the beach," I tell him.

"No, I didn't, Flora," he says, gently. "You remembered it wrong. You also think that I wrote you emails but I didn't. You wrote them to yourself. You imagined it all. I'm sorry, but I'm pleased you're safe. You ran away and we had to call Toby to bring others from the town to help us to find you."

THE MOUNTAIN

I don't want to listen to him. Something has changed in my brain and I no longer feel in love with him. I don't even know him. He is a stranger and I cannot think of a word to say to him. I care more about the people out there looking for me. I don't want anyone to get hurt because of me.

Suddenly, someone comes through the door. She has grey hair.

"Henny!" shouts Agi.

Henny looks very cold and tired but she smiles when she sees me, so I must know her, too.

There is a **gunshot** outside and I jump. The terrible sound rings out around the mountains. Everyone in the room is very nervous. I can feel it but I don't want to look at anyone. A polar bear has been killed because of me.

The door flies open and two men fall through it.

"Look!" shouts Nadia, the woman with the straight hair.

She is pointing to the window. We all look towards it and see a huge polar bear and two cubs walking calmly up the mountain.

I turn and look at Toby. "Was there another bear?" I ask.

"No, just those three," he replies. "I used my gun to scare the mother away, but they are all OK."

I smile at Toby. "Thank goodness," I say.

Then I look at the man next to Toby. He is taking off his heavy coat and underneath it is a colourful jumper.

"Dad!" I shout. He opens his arms and I run to him. I want him to hold me forever.

CHAPTER THIRTEEN
Home

I don't know where I am. I cannot think – in my mind, words come and go, but they don't fit together.

My mum and dad are talking in this room. I try to understand what they are saying.

"She's *fine*," Mum is saying.

"She's not fine," Dad says. "This is not right. It's not fair. Flora is in there – she's brave and clever. She got herself all the way to the Arctic! She can do more than you think. We can't always protect her from everything. We can't do this to her."

"She's alive and she's safe," replies Mum. "She won't be like this forever, Steve. It's just for now. I just can't lose her again. Not after losing Jacob."

"She's breathing, Annie, but she's not alive. It's not the same thing," says Dad.

I close my eyes.

———

I am sitting at a table, and there is food in front of me. I stare at it. My mum and dad are at the table, too.

"Eat your vegetables, darling," Mum says.

I eat a yellow vegetable to make her happy. I look at my hands. One of them says, **FLORA, be brave**. Mum is watching me.

"I hate that **tattoo**," Mum says to Dad. "I'm sure it gives her ideas."

I have no ideas.

———————

Now I am sitting on the sofa. Dad comes in and says that I have a visitor, then a girl walks into the room. She has dark hair and creamy skin. She is very pretty.

"Flora!" she says. "It's amazing to see you. Are you OK?"

She sits next to me on the sofa and I look at her.

"It's me – Paige. Do you remember? I'm your friend," she tells me.

"She's getting better," my dad says. "Can I get you a drink?"

"Tea, please, Mr Banks. Thanks," Paige says.

Dad leaves the room and Paige takes my hand.

"Flora, please listen to me," Paige whispers to me. "I'm sorry. I'm really sorry! I was awful to you. I blamed you for kissing Drake, when the only person to blame was Drake. Drake lied to you, Flora. You *did* kiss him on the beach. Someone took a picture and I've *seen* it! You remembered the kiss and that memory was real. You didn't imagine it, like he said, and he probably did send you all of those emails. I'm sure Drake lied about everything. You've forgotten him, haven't you? Well, it doesn't matter now. All that matters is that you got yourself to the Arctic. You're amazing, Flora, and it's awful to see you like this. Your mum is giving you lots of pills to keep you calm and quiet, and your dad is letting her do it because she is terribly sad about Jacob. But this is not you! You can't live like this."

I am staring at her and trying hard to understand. I went to the Arctic?

"Jacob said that they would do this to you," Paige continues. "Jacob loved you very much, Flora. He was wonderful, but now he's gone. He died, Flora."

I remember Jacob. He picked me up when I was little, and now he is dead. I start to cry. Paige holds me in her arms.

"Flora," Paige whispers in my ear, "do you want to get out of here and live a life again?"

I can see that she wants me to say yes, so I nod.

"I'll come and see you again tomorrow," says Paige.

———

I am on the sofa, watching television. Mum and Dad are there with me. Someone is at the front door. My dad answers it.

"Can I take Flora to look at the sea?" I hear the person say to Dad.

"That's a lovely idea, Paige," says Dad.

My friend Paige comes into the room. I remember her.

"Is it OK if Flora and I walk down to the beach together, Mrs Banks?" Paige asks Mum.

"Yes, Paige, but don't be out long," says Mum.

Paige and I walk slowly down to the shore and sit down on the sand. I love the smell of the air. She takes my hand

and looks into my eyes.

"Flora, from today, we're going to get the real you back," she begins. "The pills that your mum and dad are giving you aren't real pills any more because I changed them to sugar pills. They look like your pills but they don't actually do anything – they won't affect you in any way."

"Sugar pills," I repeat.

"Your skin will go spotty and you might feel strange for a few days – that always happens when you stop taking your pills. But after that you will start to feel better. I'm going to give you a letter now. I want you to read it and keep reading it again and again. You must keep it in a safe place, away from your parents."

Paige hands me a letter. I open it up and slowly start to read.

My little Flora,

When you're reading this, I'll be dead, and probably a ghost. If I am a ghost, I'll do my very best to keep an eye on you forever.

I have given this letter to Paige, who I hope you are now friends with again. If not, Paige better watch out for my ghost – I'm coming to get her!

Our mother and your father (my stepfather) have lied to you for seven years about how your brain was damaged. I think that it's time you knew the truth, so here it is:

When you were ten, we were all in a car accident. Our parents told you that you had a brain tumour because they couldn't bear to think about the accident again. We were on our way to a fairground called Flambards. Our parents were unhurt, but you had terrible head **injuries** and my face was badly burned. I kept my mind, and you kept your looks.

Mum was driving, and she has always blamed herself. That's why she's so protective of you. That's also why she has never been the same since. She can't bear the thought of you ever getting hurt again. That's why she makes you take all of those pills – they make you easier to control. They are not for your amnesia – there aren't actually any pills for that.

You remember things for a few hours, then you forget them. But there is a big chance that your brain could be healing because you remembered that you kissed that boy. It was the memory that was the amazing thing, not the kiss. But you knew that there was something amazing about it, so you had to run off to the Arctic and find out what it was!

And that wasn't your first adventure – you have run away before. First, you went to London by yourself, then you came to Paris to see me last year. We spent four amazing days together in Paris, and we got you the "FLORA, be brave" tattoo on your hand, to remind you to have adventures. Mum hated it!

In Paris, we went to see a **neurologist** called Joe Epstein. He was really interested in seeing you and looking at your memory damage. Mum and Dad knew about him but they didn't want his help. He still wants to help you, Flora, so Paige and I have made a plan for you to meet him again.

You are going to stop taking those pills and get your life back.

I have opened a bank account for you so you can have adventures and make a life of your own. You can do it! Paige will help you.

Live your life, Flora. Be brave.

Jacob xxx

There is too much in my head. I stare at the paper. I seem to be crying.

"Flora, I've spoken to Doctor Epstein, the neurologist, on the phone," Paige says. "He wants to meet you in Paris. He thinks that your one memory of the kiss with Drake was an 'island of memory', which could mean that your memory is getting better. We can go to Paris to meet Doctor Epstein soon, if you want to go. Do you? After that, you can decide on your next step but I'll be there with you all the way."

"I kissed a boy on a beach, and I remember it," I say.

"You did!" Paige says. "You kissed a boy on a beach. You're an adult now – you can have adventures and you can plan your own future. Your parents can't keep you here any more."

I smile at her. I don't know much about anything, but I know that I want to have adventures and get better.

"Let's go to Paris," I tell her, then I look down at my hand and say aloud: "Flora, be brave."

During-reading questions

1 Why is Flora unhappy about her white dress at the party?
2 On the beach, Flora thinks "I have nothing to lose." What does she mean by this, do you think?

1 How does Paige find out about Flora's kiss with Drake? What does Paige do after that?
2 Why doesn't Flora tell her parents about kissing Drake?

1 Why does Flora start writing her "Rules for Life"? What are they?
2 Flora can remember kissing Drake on the beach. What are the only other things that can she remember? Why is the memory of Drake's kiss so important to Flora?

1 Flora thinks that Drake is "the only person in the world now." What does she mean by this, do you think?
2 What does Flora do to make her parents believe that Paige is at home with her?

CHAPTER FIVE

1 Why does Flora go to the police station?
2 What three important things does Flora find in her parents' office?

CHAPTER SIX

1 In his email to Flora, Drake writes, "We are too far away, and you can't come here, can you?" Flora thinks that Drake would like her to go to Svalbard. Does Drake really mean that, do you think?

2 Where does Paige think that Flora is going? Where is she *really* going?

CHAPTER SEVEN

1 What does Flora buy at Oslo airport? Why does she buy it?

2 The man at the Arctic Guesthouse tells Flora not to leave town alone. Why?

CHAPTER EIGHT

1 What do we learn about Agi in this chapter?

2 How does Flora plan to find Drake?

CHAPTER NINE

1 In his email to Flora, Jacob says "You're in Penzance with your friend, aren't you? Or have you gone on another adventure?" Why does he say this, do you think? What does Flora think when she reads this?

2 What happens after Flora decides to go out for the evening?

CHAPTER TEN

1 What does Flora write in her notebook about winter in Svalbard?

2 Why does Flora suddenly change when Agi sees the satellite dishes?

CHAPTER ELEVEN

1 Why does Jacob tell Flora to stop taking her pills?
2 Drake tells Flora that he did not kiss her. Do you think Drake is telling the truth?

CHAPTER TWELVE

1 Who is Toby? How does he know Flora?
2 What is Flora worried about after she hears the gunshot? What does Flora then see out of the window of the cabin?

CHAPTER THIRTEEN

1 How does Paige know that Drake *did* kiss Flora on the beach?
2 Jacob tells Flora that she did not have a brain tumour when she was ten. How did she get amnesia?

After-reading questions

1 When Flora buys her fur coat in Penzance, how does the woman in the clothes shop know her name? Why does Flora hate that, do you think?

2 Flora's parents do not trust her to stay at home on her own. In what ways does Flora show that she can manage on her own? Think of three ways and write them down in your notebook.

3 On the boat trip, Flora sees a polar bear and her cubs. Flora thinks, "I know that that mother would do anything to protect her cubs. Anything at all." Flora's mother is also protective but she does not let Flora have any freedom. How does she do this, and why? Is this right or wrong, do you think?

4 Why did Jacob move away to Paris? What does Flora *not* remember about her relationship with Jacob?

5 Flora always has the words, "Flora, be brave" on her hand. Why are they very important to Flora? What do we learn about those words in the last chapter of the book?

Exercises

1 Who is thinking this, do you think? Write the correct name in your notebook.

> Flora   Paige's mum   Flora's dad   Paige
> Drake   Flora's mum

1 "I can't believe Flora kissed Drake! And now she thinks she loves him! I'm never speaking to her again." ....*Paige*..........

2 "I'm really worried about my son, Jacob. I must go to Paris to see him, but I hate to leave Flora." .

3 "I kissed a boy on the beach, and I can remember it!"

4 "I can't wait to get to Svalbard! I've wanted to live there since I was ten."

5 "I don't like Flora. She always needs a lot of help."

6 "I wish Flora wouldn't ask her mum about Flambards!"

CHAPTER THREE

2 Complete the first paragraph of "Flora's story" in your notebook, using the words from the box.

> since   memories   tumour   illness   memory   brain

You are 16 17 years old and you live in Penzance in Cornwall. When you were ten a ¹..........*tumour*.......... grew in your ².......... and, when you were 11, doctors took it out. Part of your ³.......... went with it. You can remember how to do things (how to make a cup of tea, how to work the shower), and you can remember your life before the ⁴.......... But ⁵.......... it happened, you have not been able to make new ⁶...........

3 **Put the words in the correct order to make sentences in your notebook.**

1 probably / Drake / has / seen / hasn't / email / now / by / my / and / answered.

Drake has probably seen my email by now and hasn't answered.

2 only / I / like / I / when / was / I / ten, / bigger. / look / did

3 ago. / parents' / My / France / landed / ten / flight / minutes / from / around

4 we / home / Jacob / still / can. / very / ill / will / is / soon / come / as / as / we / but

5 to / me / tell / is / die / but / don't / going / want / to / in / a / text. / probably / they / Jacob

6 don't / came / I / back. / why / and / Jacob / away / never / know / went

CHAPTER SIX

4 **Match the two parts of these sentences in your notebook.**

Example: 1 – c

1 My cheeks start to feel hot

2 I'm really sorry but I think that

3 I set off with my suitcase

4 I am going to fly to the Arctic

5 Paige stares at me hard for several seconds,

6 The word "Spitsbergen" is written

a to find the man who has made me remember.

b then turns and walks away.

c and I am filled with love for Drake.

d in thick black pen on my hand.

e and lock the front door behind me.

f we should stop talking to each other like this.

5 **Complete these sentences with the correct form of the verb in your notebook.**

1 Drake ....*is*................ (**be**) in Spitsbergen, and soon I ....*will be*.............. (**be**), too.

2 I .... (**read**) my notes on the journey, so right now I know what I .... (**do**).

3 This might be the first time that I .... (**ever sleep**) in a room that is not my pink bedroom.

4 Soon my parents .... (**realize**) that I .... (**not be**) at home.

5 Maybe the boys .... (**make**) all the noise.

6 "If you .... (**not find**) Drake, perhaps I .... (**see**) you here tonight," says Agi.

CHAPTER NINE

6 **Put the sentences in the correct order in your notebook.**

a .... I look up and see that everyone has left the café.

b .... At the guesthouse, the man with the beard waves at me, then he turns and walks away.

c .... I change my clothes and go out for the evening, but a man tells me that it is very early in the morning.

d .....*1*..... I find my way to the university by looking at my map, but all of the doors that I try are locked.

e .... The man with the beard from the café follows me back to my guesthouse.

f .... I decide to find somewhere warm to sit and write a reply to Jacob.

g .... I look in the bedroom mirror and see that my eyes look different and my skin is spotty.

CHAPTERS TEN AND ELEVEN

7 **Write the questions to these answers in your notebook.**

1 *Where do Flora and Agi go together?*
  They go on a boat tour.
2 They see a polar bear and two cubs.
3 She sees satellite dishes at the top of the mountain.
4 She tells Flora that he has a girlfriend called Nadia.
5 She rows to the cabin across the water.
6 Flora feels very angry when Drake says that she is lying.

CHAPTER TWELVE

8 **Write the correct word in your notebook.**

1 ianbc — I can't go back to town, so I run up the mountain behind the ....*cabin*...........
2 rfnezegi — I want to stay here, alone in this .... place, forever.
3 ostp — The man has a beard and a brown .... on his face.
4 emnasai — "Yes, you have ...., but you are alive!" the man says.
5 nusohgt — There is a .... outside and I jump.
6 ktahn sgodonse — I smile at Toby and say, " ....

91

9 **Are these sentences true or false? Write the correct answers in your notebook.**

1 Flora has a "Flora, be brave" T-shirt. ...._false_................
2 There is a picture of Drake and Paige kissing on the beach.
3 Flora's mum is terribly sad about Jacob.
4 Flora's skin goes white when she stops taking her pills.
5 Jacob's face was badly burned in the car accident.
6 Flora met a neurologist called Joe Epstein in Svalbard.

Project work

1 In the café in Longyearbyen (see Chapter Nine), Flora replies to Jacob's first email to her. She says, "I write everything that has happened and everything that I feel in my email – I don't leave anything out." Write that email from Flora to Jacob.

2 Imagine that you are Flora or Jacob. Write a diary of one of the "four amazing days" you spent together in Paris. Mention one of the following events:
   • Flora surprising Jacob when she arrived
   • Seeing the Eiffel Tower
   • Meeting Doctor Joe Epstein

3 Look online to find out more about the Arctic and Svalbard, then make a poster for the boat trip that Flora goes on with Agi.

4 What happens to Flora after the story, do you think? Write another chapter for the book that looks at Flora's life three years later.

Glossary

account (n.)
when you have agreed to use
something that a company, bank etc.
gives to people. For example, you
send and get messages in an email
account. You put your money into and
take it out of a bank *account*.

amazed (adj.)
very surprised

anterograde amnesia (n.)
when a person cannot remember
new information because the part of
their *brain* which makes *memories* has
been damaged

bay (n.)
a place where the sea goes into the
land and makes a circle. There are
often boats in a *bay*.

blame (v.)
to say that a person did
something wrong

brain (n.)
the part inside your head that
controls how you think, feel, move,
etc.

cabin (n.)
a small house in the mountains or
forest. A *cabin* is often made
of wood.

cosy (adj.)
comfortable and warm

cub (n.)
a young animal. Young *polar bears* are
called *cubs*.

darling (n.)
You sometimes say *darling* when you
speak to someone that you love.

deck (n.)
one of the floors in a boat, bus
or plane. The top *deck* of a boat is
usually outside.

fairground (n.)
a place where people ride in
machines for fun. The machines go
up and down or round and round
very fast.

find out (phr. v.)
to discover a piece of information for
the first time

flight (n.)
a journey in a plane

freedom (n.)
being able to do the things that you
want to do

freezing (adj.)
extremely cold

fur (n.)
the hair that covers an animal.
A *fur* coat is a coat made of *fur*.

guesthouse (n.)
a small hotel or someone's home
where you can pay to stay the night

gunshot (n.)
the action of using a gun, or the sound that using a gun makes

handbag (n.)
a small bag for carrying things like money, keys, etc.

heal (v.)
If a person or a part of a person's body *heals*, or if someone or something *heals* them, they were ill or hurt and then they become well again.

injury (n.)
when a part of a person's body is hurt or damaged, usually because of an accident

land (v.)
to go down to the ground after a journey in a plane

landscape (n.)
the things that you can see in a large area of land

lip (n.)
the two parts at the edge of your mouth that you use to kiss someone

lipstick (n.)
colour that you put on your *lips*

memory (n.)
1) something that you remember from the past
2) your ability to remember things

neurologist (n.)
a doctor for illnesses which affect the nervous system (= the way your *brain* works with your body so that you can feel pain and move different parts of your body)

panic (v.)
to suddenly feel very worried in a way that stops you from thinking clearly or knowing what to do

passport (n.)
a document that has your photograph and shows your name and when you were born. You need a *passport* to travel to a foreign country.

polar bear (n.)
a large white bear. *Polar bears* live in the Arctic (= the most north part of the Earth).

Post-it note (n.)
a small piece of paper that you can write on and then *stick* to other things to help you remember something

prepare (v.)
to get ready to do something, or to make someone or something ready to do something. If you *prepare* a meal, you make food ready for people to eat.

pretend (v.)
to make people think that something is true when it is not

protect (v.); **protective** (adj.)
to look after someone or something
and stop bad things from happening
to them. If you are *protective* of
someone, you often try to
protect them.

recognize (v.)
You *recognize* someone when you
know who they are because you
have seen them before.

reindeer (n.)
a large brown animal with big horns
(= long hard things that grow out of
its head). We usually say *reindeer* for
two or more of them.

relationship (n.)
1) when two people are special
friends, love each other and have sex
2) the way two people are when they
are together. If they like each other,
they have a good *relationship*.

remind (v.)
to make someone remember
something or someone

row (v.)
to make a boat move through water
by using oars (= long sticks)

rule (n.)
something that you must or must
not do

satellite (n.);
satellite dish (n.);
satellite station (n.)
Satellites are sent into space to send
pictures and information to Earth.
Information from *satellites* can be
sent to a round thing on Earth
called a *satellite dish*. A *satellite station*
is a place where special machines
are used to follow *satellites* and get
information from them.

screen (n.)
the flat, square part of a television
or computer where you see pictures
or words

seal (n.)
a large animal that lives in or near
the sea and eats fish. *Seals* are
usually grey with big black eyes,
and they live in colder parts of the
world.

set off (phr. v.)
to start a journey

shore (n.)
the land at the edge of a sea or
lake (= an area of water with land
around it)

spot (n.); **spotty** (adj.)
a *spot* is a small round mark on your
skin. If a person is *spotty*, they have a
lot of *spots* on their skin.

stepfather (n.)
a man who has married your
mother but is not your real father

stick (v.)
to attach one thing to another thing

suitcase (n.)
a large, square bag that you put
your clothes in when you travel. It
often has wheels.

tattoo (n.)
a picture or some words that have
been drawn on your skin and stay
there forever

thank goodness (phr.)
You say *thank goodness* when you are
happy that something bad did not
happen or that something bad has
stopped.

tour (n.)
1) a short visit around a place
2) a journey to see a lot of different
places

tumour (n.)
a group of cells (= the smallest
living parts of the body) in a person
or animal's body that are not
growing in a normal way. A person
can become very ill or die because
of a *tumour*.

work out (phr. v.)
1) If you *work* something *out*, you
understand or decide something
after thinking carefully.
2) If something *works out*, it develops
in a positive way.